Note to parents, carers and teachers

Read it yourself is a series of modern stories, favourite characters and traditional tales written in a simple way for children who are learning to read. The books can be read independently or as part of a guided reading session.

Each book is carefully structured to include many high-frequency words vital for first reading. The sentences on each page are supported closely by pictures to help with understanding, and to offer lively details to talk about.

The books are graded into four levels that progressively introduce wider vocabulary and longer stories as a reader's ability and confidence grows.

Ideas for use

- Begin by looking through the book and talking about the pictures. Has your child heard this story before?

- Help your child with any words he does not know, either by helping him to sound them out or supplying them yourself.

- Developing readers can be concentrating so hard on the words that they sometimes don't fully grasp the meaning of what they're reading. Answering the puzzle questions on pages 30 and 31 will help with understanding.

For more information and advice on Read it yourself and book banding, visit **www.ladybird.com/readityourself**

Book
Band
7

Level 2 is ideal for children who have received some reading instruction and can read short, simple sentences with help.

Special features:

Frequent repetition of main story words and phrases

Short, simple sentences

The king took the girl to a room full of straw.

"You must spin this straw into gold," the king said.

The girl began to cry. "I cannot do this," she said.

8

9

Large, clear type

A funny little man came into the room.

"If you give me your necklace, I will help you," said the man.

"Yes," said the girl. "I will give you my necklace."

Careful match between story and pictures

10

11

Educational Consultant: Geraldine Taylor
Book Banding Consultant: Kate Ruttle

A catalogue record for this book is available from the British Library

Published by Ladybird Books Ltd
80 Strand, London, WC2R 0RL
A Penguin Company

005

ISBN: 978-0-72327-298-4

Printed in China

Rumpelstiltskin

Illustrated by Marina Le Ray

One day, a poor man took his daughter to see the king.

"My daughter can spin straw into gold," said the poor man.

The king took the girl to a room full of straw.

"You must spin this straw into gold," the king said.

The girl began to cry.
"I cannot do this," she said.

A funny little man came into the room.

"If you give me your necklace, I will help you," said the man.

"Yes," said the girl. "I will give you my necklace."

The next day, the room was full of gold.

So the king gave the girl more straw to spin into gold.

The funny little man came into the room.

"If you give me your ring, I will help you," said the funny little man.

"Yes," said the girl. "I will give you my ring."

The next day, the room
was full of gold.

The king gave the girl more
straw. "If you can spin this
straw into gold," he said,
"you will be my queen."

The funny little man came into the room.

"If you give me your first child, I will help you," said the funny little man.

"Yes," said the girl. "I will give you my first child."

The next day, the room was full of gold.

The king married the girl. Soon, they had a child.

The funny little man came to see the queen.

"If you cannot guess my name," said the man, "you must give me your child."

The queen began to cry.

The queen sent her men to find every name they could.

But she could not guess the name of the funny little man.

Then one man saw the
funny little man singing:

*"The queen will never
win my game,
For Rumpelstiltskin
is my name!"*

The man went to tell
the queen.

The next day the queen
said to the funny little man,
"Is your name...
Rumpelstiltskin?"

And the funny little man
was so cross, he ran away
and was never seen again.

How much do you remember about the story of Rumpelstiltskin? Answer these questions and find out!

- What does the poor man say the girl can do?

- Who helps her to do this?

- Can you name two things the girl gave the funny little man?

- How does the queen find out Rumpelstiltskin's name?

Look at the pictures and match them to the story words.

gold

king

straw

Rumpelstiltskin

girl

Read it yourself with Ladybird

Tick the books you've read!

For beginner readers who can read short, simple sentences with help.

Level **2**

☐ ☐

☐ ☐ ☐ ☐ ☐ ☐ ☐

☐ ☐ ☐ ☐ ☐ ☐ ☐

For more confident readers who can read simple stories with help.

Level **3**

☐ ☐

☐ ☐ ☐ ☐ ☐ ☐ ☐

The Read it yourself with Ladybird app is now available for iPad, iPhone and iPod touch

App also available on Android devices